For my godchildren – Jannis, Ann, Ellen and Lina
~ K S

For Mum, Dad, James and everyone else
behind the scenes
~ L H

This edition produced 2008 for BOOKS ARE FUN LTD
1680 Hwy 1 North, Fairfield, Iowa, IA 52556

Copyright © 2005 by Good Books, Intercourse, PA 17534
International Standard Book Number: 978-1-84506-912-4

Library of Congress Catalog Card Number: 2005002667

Text copyright © Kenneth Steven 2005
Illustrations copyright © Magi Publications 2005

Original edition published in English by Little Tiger Press,
an imprint of Magi Publications, London, England, 2005.

Printed in China

Library of Congress Cataloging-in-Publication Data is available for this title.

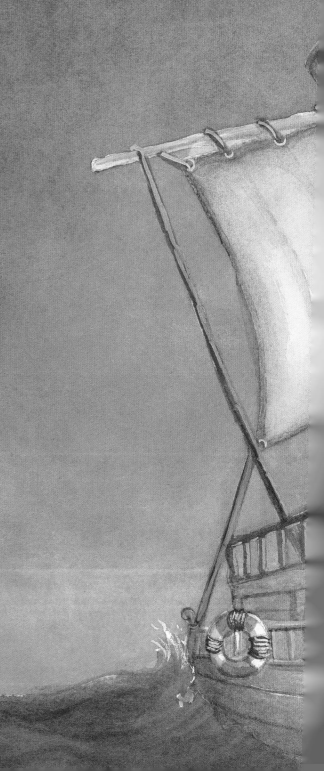

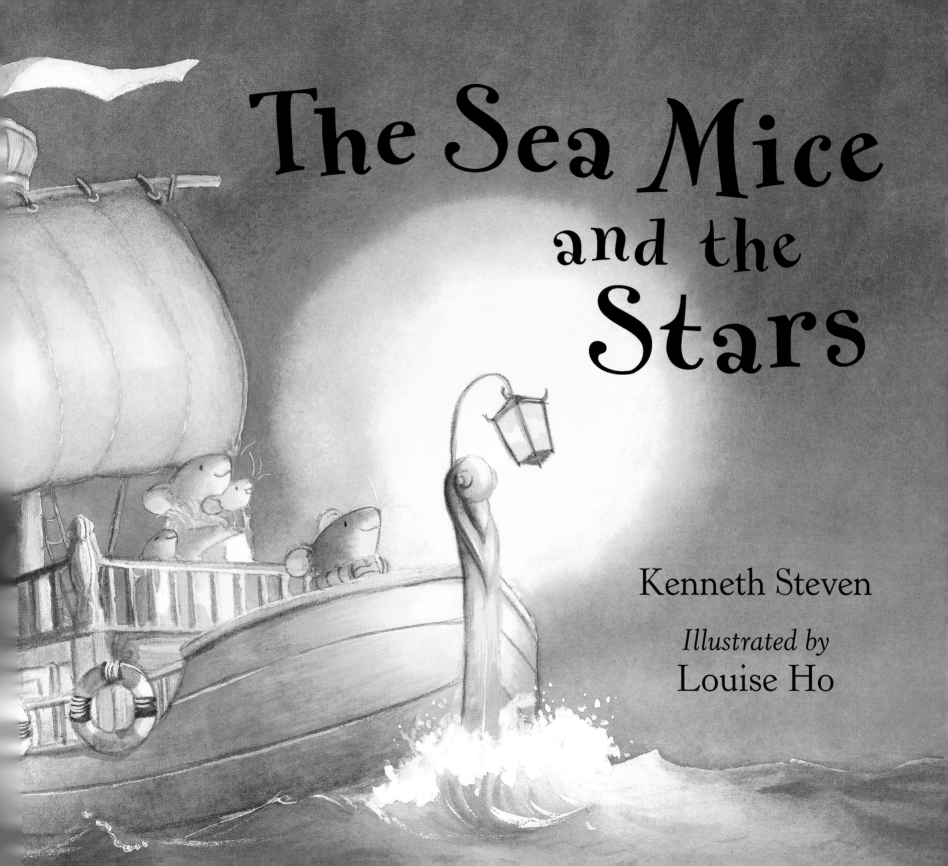

The Sea Mice
and the
Stars

Kenneth Steven

Illustrated by
Louise Ho

THE SEA URCHIN

It was winter and the young sea mice
were fast asleep in their boat *The Sea Urchin*.
Outside, snow was falling soft as petals.

Ashenteen woke suddenly.

"Come quickly, little one," her mother Filidore was whispering. "There's something you must see!"

Racing her brother Willabee to the deck, Ashenteen squeaked in amazement. The sky was filled with shooting lights.

"What's happening to the stars?" Ashenteen cried. "Where are they going?"

"Every year," said Uncle Trumble, "as winter comes, there is a shower of falling stars. These stars are pieces of magic, sent to the sea mice to keep us safe. It is our family's task to collect them. We share them with the village mice and save some to guide our boat."

Wrapped in their cozy scarves, the mice set off into the night. The waves leaped and danced as they rowed to the shore, and Ashenteen trembled with excitement.

"You must be brave, Pippy," she whispered to her favorite toy. "We're going on a very important journey."

At the shore the village mice rushed to welcome them.

"Here are your baskets, Mr. Trumble!" said Stigmore.

"But you must hurry, there's a terrible storm coming!"

Uncle Trumble, Filidore, Willabee and Ashenteen
struggled up into the snowy hills. The wind howled
around them and snowflakes whirled through the
dark sky. Ashenteen slipped her paw into Willabee's.
This was their very own adventure.

At long last the mice reached a clearing. There lay
hundreds of stars, sparkling like precious jewels in
the snow.

Willabee gasped, his eyes shining.

Ashenteen lifted a glowing shape between both paws.
"Look, Mom!" she squeaked.

"Quickly now!" called Uncle Trumble. "The storm is
getting worse! We must gather all of the stars and go back!"

Ashenteen scampered to
and fro, collecting more
and more stars.

Further and further
she searched, determined
to collect every single one.

"Nearly there," she said, stretching
up into the branches of a tree.

At last she picked the final star from the ground.

"Hello, little star," she murmured, cradling it
gently. All around was darkness, but her basket
was full to the brim with light.

"We did it!" she whispered proudly.

Filidore put down her basket and looked around for the other mice. "Willabee? Ashenteen?" she called.

"Mom! Mom!" Willabee raced up. "I've found Pippy!" he squeaked. "Ashenteen must have dropped him! I can't find her anywhere!"

"Ashenteen? Ashenteen!" the sea mice called, but there
was no answer.

They peered into the dark and snow. Willabee shivered.
What if Ashenteen was lost forever? But just then he saw
something flickering faintly in the dark.

"Ashenteen!" Willabee cried. The mice rushed to the glowing light of her basket.

"Thank goodness, you're safe!" Filidore said, hugging her youngest mouse close.

Ashenteen beamed with happiness. "I collected every single star I could find!" she murmured.

"Well done, my brave girl," said Filidore proudly.

Uncle Trumble led the mice back through
the wild wind and snow. Ashenteen and Willabee
stumbled on and on, their paws icy cold. At last
they saw the village ahead of them and heard an
excited cry, "You're back, safe and sound!"

The villagers welcomed the sea mice
and wrapped them in warm blankets.
Proudly the mice shared out the stars
they had collected—one for every home.

Then the mice had a great celebration. There were spicy hot drinks that made Ashenteen's nose tingle, and singing and dancing that never seemed to end.

"This is the most exciting night ever!" Ashenteen
whispered to Willabee as they nibbled on special
star-shaped cookies, still warm from the oven.

Later the sleepy mice rowed home. The sea was quiet now, and all around the bay the bright new stars shone in the darkness.

Tucked up tight in her bed, Ashenteen gazed at her own special star, blazing out from the prow of the boat. "Good night, Willabee," she whispered, then fell fast asleep, dreaming of the day's great adventure.